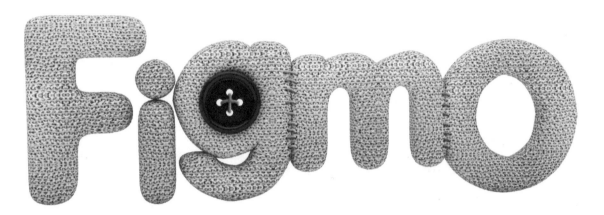

Figmo

A Tale of a Boy and His Blanket

Written by
AJ Frank

Illustrated by
Eduardo Paj

hardcover ISBN: 978-1-7354036-0-1
softcover ISBN: 978-1-7354036-2-5

Published in association with Bear With Us Productions

For "Mom"

A short time ago
there once lived a boy.
He was five years old,
his name, Stephen Roy.

Most called him "Buddy" instead of his name. Except for his Grandma, who'd have none of that game.

Blond hair and brown eyes,
he was a sprite of a lad.
And everyone said
he looked just like his dad.

Wherever he'd go,
his blanket he'd bring.
It was soft as the clouds,
and as green as the *spring*.

As wide as the ocean
and as long as the wind.
He could easily use it
to shade his new friends.

He sleeps with it, eats with it.
It rides in the car.
There's never a time
when his blanket's not far.

He plays with it always,
even out where it's muddy.
'Til his Momma cries out,
"My garden, oh Buddy!"

"Get out of that mud,
just look at your shirt!
And look at your blanket,
it's covered in dirt!"

In the tub she sent Buddy,
in the washer his pal.
Where a clean Buddy waited,
wrapped up in a towel.

One day Buddy woke,
and his blanket was gone!
He searched the whole house,
even out on the lawn.

As he entered the kitchen
through the creaky screen door,
he noticed his Dad
was scrubbing the floor.

"Oh *no*!" he exclaimed.
"My blanket's a rag!"
It was torn into pieces
and stuffed in a bag.

Buddy cried through the day
and into the night.
He tossed and he turned
filled with terror and fright.

For only he knew,
that under his bed,
lived monsters and goblins
that filled him with dread.

$\mathcal{N}$ext morning to soothe him,
Dad gave him a gift.
In hopes it'd give Buddy's
sweet spirit a lift.

$\mathcal{H}$e fought hard to smile,
but had quivering lips.
So Dad picked him up
saying, "Let's take a trip."

$\mathcal{T}$o Grandma's they went.
She didn't live far.
But still far enough
that they drove in the car.

As they drove up the drive,
Grandma waited outside.
With a wave she asked Buddy,
"How was the ride?"

Buddy ran up to greet her
and jumped in her arms.
"How's my Stephen?" she asked,
with her sweet Grandma charm.

"I'm Buddy," he said,
with a sly little grin.
"You're Stephen to me,
this game you won't win."

He kissed her and asked,
"Have a present for me?"
She giggled and thought,
"I might, let me see."

"Go sit on the couch
my cute little man.
I'll bring it right out,
as fast as I can."

When Grandma returned,
Buddy shrieked with surprise.
He couldn't believe
his very own eyes.

From her outstretched arms,
she held out a bunny,
with long floppy ears,
that made it look funny.

"My blanket!" he cried,
with joy and delight.
He squeezed it and hugged it,
and held it real tight.

"That's right, little fella,
it's your blanket, that's true.
I stitched each little piece
to make this for you."

"What is his name?"
he asked with a smile.
"Well, that's up to you!"
So, he thought for a while.

"I'll call him Figmo,"
he said after a pause.
"Why Figmo?" Gran asked.
His reply, "Just because!"

"Then Figmo it is,
my sweet little Prince.
Now go out and play,
staying inside the fence."

*H*e ran and he skipped
with his new little friend,
staying inside the fence
to play and pretend.

"*I*'ll not need to worry
about monsters again.
With you by my side,
we surely will win."

When it came time to go,
they ran in from the lawn.
Buddy sat on the couch
and let out a yawn.

"You tired, young Prince?"
Grandma said with a smile.
"Before you both go,
let's rock for a while."

He ran to her lap
and snuggled her side.
She rocked them both gently,
gleaming with pride.

"Such a sweet little Prince.
You should never know fear.
May this gift keep you strong
in faith, my sweet dear."

The End

CPSIA information can be obtained
at www.ICGtesting.com
Printed in the USA
BVHW020952140920
588774BV00004B/43

* 9 7 8 1 7 3 5 4 0 3 6 0 1 *